The Day Snuffy Had the Sniffles

By Linda Lee Maifair
Illustrated by Tom Brannon

This educational book was created in cooperation with the Children's Television Workshop, producers of Sesame Street. Children do not have to watch the television show to benefit from this book. Workshop revenues from this product will be used to help support CTW educational projects.

A SESAME STREET/GOLDEN PRESS BOOK

Published by Western Publishing Company, Inc., in conjunction with Children's Television Workshop.

Oscar the Grouch popped up out of his can just in time to see Big Bird skipping down Sesame Street. "Go away, Bird!" Oscar grumbled. "All that cheerfulness will ruin my day. Besides, it's time to collect the trash. I'm too busy to talk to you."

"That's OK, Oscar," Big Bird said. "I'm in a big hurry to get to Snuffy's house so I can cheer him up. He has the sniffles."

"Grouches don't know anything about cheering anybody up," said Oscar, "but we do know a lot about the sniffles. I have just the thing for you to take to old snuffle-nose. Wait here!"

Before Big Bird could say anything, Oscar disappeared into his can, banging the lid shut behind him.

Big Bird was waiting impatiently for Oscar when
Cookie Monster came along.

"What's the matter?" Cookie asked Big Bird. "Somebody eat all your cookies?"

"Worse than that," Big Bird said. "Snuffy's got the sniffles and can't come out to play. I'm waiting for Oscar. He has a surprise for me to take to Snuffy."

"Cheer-up surprise?" said Cookie Monster. "Wait here!" He left in such a rush that he nearly ran into Bert.

As soon as Bert heard that Snuffy had the sniffles, he told Big Bird, "I know just the thing to cheer up a sniffly Snuffle-upagus. Wait here!" He dashed into 123 Sesame Street before Big Bird could open his beak to say one word.

Big Bird plopped down on the steps next to Oscar's can. "At this rate I'll *never* get to see Snuffy!" he said. He tapped his foot. He stood up. He paced back and forth. He sat down. Then he did the same thing all over again.

Just when Big Bird decided that he couldn't wait one second longer, Bert ran down the steps and handed him a large shoe box. Big Bird peeked inside.

"It's my bottle-cap collection," Bert said proudly. "You can lend it to Snuffy. It will give him something fascinating to look at while he's sick in bed. There's nothing more exciting than bottle caps, except maybe paper clips."

Before Big Bird could answer, Cookie Monster
came back. Huffing and puffing, he held out
a slightly dented cookie tin.

"Gee, thanks, Cookie," Big Bird said. He tugged
at the lid. "I just know Snuffy will enjoy all these...
COOKIE CRUMBS?"

Cookie Monster shrugged. "Well," he said, "it's
the thought that counts." He brushed chocolate
chips and cookie crumbs off his tummy. "Sure
cheered me up!" he said.

Just then Oscar popped back up. "Here, Bird," he said, "the perfect thing for old Sniffy." He placed a jar of something lumpy and green on top of the shoe box and cookie tin.

"It's an old Grouch family recipe, handed down from grandgrouch to momgrouch. It's sure to cure even Snuffle-upagus-sized sniffles—sardine-and-sauerkraut soup!" Oscar said.

Bert and Cookie Monster held their noses.
"Blecch!" they said.

"You'd better get a move on, Bird," said Oscar.
"Can't let that soup get too warm. Sardine-and-
sauerkraut soup only tastes its worst when it's
good and cold."

Juggling the shoe box, the cookie tin, and the smelly Grouch soup, Big Bird started off again. He was glad to be on his way to Snuffy's at last. He got as far as the library when he met Betty Lou.

As soon as she heard where Big Bird was going, Betty Lou said, "I know just the thing to cheer up Snuffy. Come on!"

Before Big Bird could make a peep, Betty Lou took him up the steps and into the library.

"Everybody's sure in a hurry to make me wait!"
said Big Bird, looking around. Finally Betty Lou
came back.

She balanced a thick book on top of Big Bird's
bundles. "Here's an animal picture book for Snuffy
to look at all by himself. And here's a monster
storybook for his mother to read to him." She piled
an even thicker book on top of the first one.
"There's nothing like a good book to cheer you up!"
said Betty Lou.

Big Bird's arms were so full, he couldn't wave good-bye to Betty Lou. "It's a good thing Snuffy's cave isn't far!" he said.

"What do you have there, Big Bird?" the Count called from his castle window. "One shoe box! One tin! One jar! Two books! Wonderful!"

Big Bird told the Count why he was in a hurry. "I have just the thing for your friend," the Count said. "Wait there!"

After what seemed like hours to Big Bird, the
Count came out of his castle and handed him a box
of tissues.

"Snuffy can count them and count them as much
as he pleases, and they'll come in handy whenever
he sneezes!" the Count said.

Crinkled, wrinkled tissues stuck out of the box.

"I counted them myself. There are two hundred
tissues!" the Count said.

Big Bird tiptoed quietly past Gladys' barn.

"My, my, you do have your hands full," said Gladys the cow.

"These are surprises for Snuffy," Big Bird explained. "He has the sniffles. I've been trying all morning to go cheer him up."

"Well, any cow knows there's only one way to do that," Gladys said. "Wait here!"

"Not again!" Big Bird said. But Gladys had already trotted into the barn.

Gladys' cheer-up present turned out to be a pint of ice cream. It was getting soft and soggy in the noontime sun. "Nothing puts you in a good *mooood* like ice cream," Gladys said. Her bell tinkled as she balanced the squishy ice-cream carton on top of the wrinkled tissues and the books and the jar and the empty cookie tin and the shoe box.

Big Bird watched the sticky pink drops fall onto his toes.

"It's strawberry," Gladys explained.

At last Big Bird made it to Snuffy's cave without dropping a single present.

He pushed open the front door with his foot.

Then he had a terrible thought. "I brought all these presents for Snuffy and not a single one of them is from *me*! I forgot to bring Snuffy a present!"

Big Bird sighed a deep sigh and shifted the slippery pile of presents. "I hope Snuffy won't be too disappointed," he said.

And there was Snuffy, propped up on huge stuffed
pillows in his Snuffle-upagus-sized bed. On a tray in
front of him was a glass of orange juice, a box of
cough drops, a coloring book, and a box of crayons.
Snuffy had an ice pack on his head and a
thermometer sticking out of his mouth.

Mrs. Snuffle-upagus took the thermometer out of Snuffy's mouth and studied it for a moment. "No more fever!" she said.

She took a bottle and measured the thick orange sniffles medicine into a spoon. Snuffy swallowed it all.

Mrs. Snuffle-upagus gave him a big hug. "Cheer up, Son," she told him. "You'll be out of that bed in no time!"

"Uh-oh!" Big Bird said. The cheer-up surprises were slipping from his grasp.

"Ah...Ah...CHOO!" Snuffy sneezed a gigantic snuffle sneeze that rattled everything in the room. The presents crashed to the floor!

"Oh, dear!" said Mrs. Snuffle-upagus.

Big Bird stood in the doorway, feeling sadder than ever. How could he cheer up Snuffy now?

Snuffy blew his snuffle on a handkerchief the size of a tablecloth. Then he smiled at Big Bird. "Oh, Bird," he snuffled, "how did you guess what I wanted to cheer me up?"

Big Bird stared at the mess on the floor. "What's that, Snuffy?" he asked. "The bottle caps? The cookie crumbs? The melted ice cream? Or the sardine-and-sauerkraut soup?"

"No, Bird," said Snuffy, "a visit from *you*!"

That cheered up Big Bird, too!